For Helen, my ever
amusing muse, with love – P. B.

For Alvie, Ted and Ramona – B.I.

This paperback edition first published in 2018 by Andersen Press Ltd.
First published in Great Britain in 2016 by
Andersen Press Ltd., 20 Vauxhall Bridge Road, London SW1V 2SA.
Text copyright © Paul Bright, 2016. Illustration copyright © Bruce Ingman, 2016.
The rights of Paul Bright and Bruce Ingman to be identified as the author
and illustrator of this work have been asserted by them in accordance
with the Copyright, Designs and Patents Act, 1988.
All rights reserved.
Colour separated in Switzerland by Photolitho AG, Zürich.
Printed and bound in China.

1 3 5 7 9 10 8 6 4 2

British Library Cataloguing
in Publication Data available.
ISBN 978 1 78344 501 1

FSC
www.fsc.org

MIX
Paper from
responsible sources
FSC® C012700

Paul Bright   Bruce Ingman

The HOLE StoRy

ANDERSEN PRESS

In a land of strange happenings, far, far away,
lived two holes, Hamish and Hermione.

Their home was a chunk of Swiss cheese,
on a plate, in the kitchen, in the royal palace.

One day, a family of mice came along and ate all the cheese.

The cook chased the mice away, but now
the two holes had nowhere to live.

"That cheese was getting stale anyway," said
Hamish Hole. "Let's leave this dreary
kitchen and search for a new home.
A place where holes can be useful."

The King was in his dressing room when he let out a cry.

"Oh no! There's a hole in my sock – I can't let my people see the royal hairy legs."

He called for the royal seamstress to darn his sock...

but by the time she arrived, Hamish Hole had gone.

The Queen was in her boudoir
when she let out a shriek.

"Oh no! There's
a hole in my
knickers – I
can't let the
people see my
royal pink
bottom."

She called for her
maid to mend her
knickers...

but by the time she arrived,
Hermione Hole had disappeared.

The Princess was riding her bicycle in the palace gardens when –

thump!
thump!
bump!

She flew over the handlebars and landed in the royal compost heap.

"Oh no! I've got turnip tops in my tiara and there's a hole in my tyre!"

She called for the repair man to patch her tyre, but by the time he arrived, Hamish Hole was nowhere to be seen.

The Prince was rowing his boat on the palace lake when water came gushing in.

"Oh no! There's a hole in my boat – it's going to sink!" He swam to the shore, soaked and soggy, clutching his crown.

But by the time he examined his boat,
Hermione Hole had vanished.

"I've been in a royal sock and a royal bike," said Hamish.
"I've been in a bag and a boot and a bucket."

"I've even been in a red balloon that burst with an enormous BANG!

But everybody just seemed grumpy."

"I've been in a pair
of royal knickers
and a royal boat,"
said Hermione.
"I've been in a COat
and a Cart."

"I've even been in a custard jug,
but nobody was pleased to see me."

"Everyone thinks we're a nuisance," said Hamish. "But holes
can be useful too." Then he yawned a big, holey yawn.

"Let's find somewhere dark and quiet to sleep," said Hermione.
"Perhaps we'll find a useful home tomorrow."

Early the next morning, the royal carpenter was mending
a chair. He searched in his dark, quiet wood store.
"This piece is no good for a chair leg," he said.
"Here's a hole... and another one. What a nuisance."

But then he had a thought. "Maybe I can use this wood for something special."

So he cut and carved and smoothed the wood into two beautiful flutes, with a hole for the mouthpiece and holes for the fingers to play.

When he was finished
the royal carpenter gave
one to the Prince and
one to the Princess.
They were so, so
pleased.

The King and Queen lay
side by side in their big, royal bed.

"I hope you have no more holes in
your socks, my dear?" said the Queen.
"Not one my precious," said the King. "I hope
you have no more holes in your knickers?"
"None at all," said the Queen. "Those
pesky holes won't bother us again."
"I hope you're right," said the King.
"But what's that noise?"

In their own bedroom the prince and princess
were practising with their new flutes.

And if the flutes squeaked now and again, then maybe,
just maybe, two very useful holes were squeaking with delight
in their wonderful new home.